TIMOTHY
and the STRONG PYJAMAS

This is the story of
Timothy
Smallbeast.
He wasn't big.
And he wasn't strong.
(But he really,
really wished he was.)

A superhero adventure by
Viviane Schwarz

ALISON GREEN BOOKS

This is Timothy!

This is his best friend,
Monkey!

And these are his
favourite pyjamas!

Every evening, before he goes to bed,
Timothy tries to make himself stronger.

He drinks a big mug of fortified milk and crunches up three extra-tough cookies.

He does some exercises.

Then he thinks **STRONG** thoughts.

Doing all that exercise is tough on your pyjamas.

"Timothy," said his mother one evening,
"these pyjamas are a disgrace.
We must buy you some new ones."

"But these are my favourite pyjamas,"
said Timothy. "And they don't sell favourite pyjamas
in the shops, they only sell new ones.
Can't you fix them for me? Please?"

So Timothy's mother fixed them for him.

She used the **strongest thread**,

and sewed them **three** times over and **crosswise** to be sure.

She sewed on lots of **sturdy patches**.

She sewed on **six** very red **buttons**,

and an extra **secret** button on the inside.

Timothy was very pleased. "Thank you!" he said. Then he picked Monkey up, and trotted upstairs to bed.

You are wearing the PATCHES of POWER and the BUTTONS of BRAVENESS.

Timothy's mother
had fixed his pyjamas so well
that they were now

Super Strong Pyjamas.

Timothy tried his strength out **very carefully.**

He was really,

extremely,

mightily,

amazingly

STRONG.

Now you are ready to become a hero.

Next morning, Timothy asked his mother
if he could wear his pyjamas all day.
Because it was the weekend,
she said he could.

"Now finish your breakfast,
so you grow up
big and strong!"

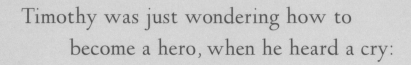

Timothy was just wondering how to become a hero, when he heard a cry:

Somebody help

eeeeee!!!

An elephant lady
had fallen
off a cliff!

What on earth was she doing
picking berries up there?

He helped . . .

An old lady . . .

a princess . . .

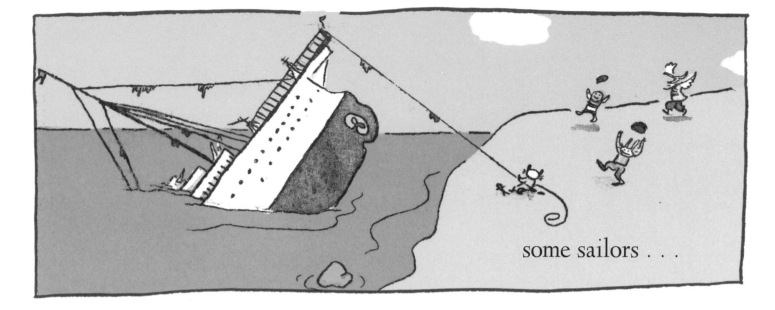

some sailors . . .

a zookeeper . . .

SPEED of the falling star!

and a kitten.

You have done well!

At last it was time to go home.

They were almost home,
when they found a **tired bear** crying in the street.
"I can't find the forest," said the bear. "I need to go to sleep for the
winter, but I've lost my way, and now I'm too tired to walk."
"Don't cry," said Timothy. "I'll carry you home."

Now it really was time to go home. "Come on, Monkey," said Timothy.
But Monkey had gone!

Oh, no, he hadn't! He was stuck underneath the bear!
"Don't worry!" said Timothy. "The bear may be fast asleep, but I'll
lift him up with my **super strength**, and pull you out."

But when Timothy tried to pull Monkey out,
his pyjamas caught on one of the bear's claws, and with a great . . .

His pyjamas were not **super strong** any more!

They were just an old pair of patchy, raggedy pyjamas.

And the bear wouldn't wake up until spring time!

"Oh no!" sobbed Timothy.
"My monkey is being hibernated on by a bear,
and I can't go to sleep without him!
And now I'm not strong any more because
my pyjamas are torn, and I'm only small
and I'm all alone in the forest!"

"That's no good!" said a voice.
It was the Elephant Lady!

She trumpeted a distress signal,
so loud it could be heard
for miles and miles around:

HELP TIMOTHY!

And here they all come!

Everyone Timothy had helped today:
the old lady, the princess,
the sailors, the zookeeper
and the kitten.

They all joined together and . . .

"Thank you!" said Timothy.
"Time to go home," said the Elephant Lady.
"I'll give you a lift."

Timothy's mother shook her head
when she saw the state of his pyjamas.
"What have you been up to?" she said.

And as Timothy
fell fast asleep with Monkey,
his mother fixed his pyjamas
better than ever.

ADVENTURE

THE END

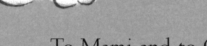

To Mami and to Omi

First published in the UK in 2007 by Alison Green Books
An imprint of Scholastic Children's Books
Euston House, 24 Eversholt Street
London NW1 1DB, UK
A division of Scholastic Ltd
London – New York – Toronto – Sydney – Auckland
Mexico City – New Delhi – Hong Kong

HB 10-digit ISBN: 0 439 94356 6
HB 13-digit ISBN: 978 0 439943 56 7
PB 10-digit ISBN: 0 439 94440 6
PB 13-digit ISBN: 978 0 439944 40 3

1 3 5 7 9 8 6 4 2

Printed in Singapore

The right of Viviane Schwarz to be identified as the author and illustrator of this work
has been asserted by her in accordance with the Copyright, Designs and Patents Act, 1988.

Papers used by Scholastic Children's Books are made from wood grown in sustainable forests.

10.7.06

For my husband Kalle and my daughter Kwezi.
And for my grandmother Anna, who inspired me in so many ways
and told me these stories.

Published by University of KwaZulu-Natal Press
(formerly University of Natal Press)
Private Bag X01
Scottsville, 3209
South Africa
Email: books@ukzn.ac.za
Website: www.ukznpress.co.za

First edition 2003
Second edition 2004

ISBN 1-86914-061-3

Editor: Elana Bregin
Layout and Design: Flying Ant Designs
Cover Illustration: Kalle Becker

Printed and bound by Interpak Books, Pietermaritzburg